One day, when our grandson Rory was a baby, he was lying on the floor surrounded by his family –
his parents, his auntie and uncle, two dogs and a cat, and his grandparents (that's us).
This image stayed in my mind, and was the seed for *Let's Go, Baby-o!*

From the beginning, babies enter into a world of people, animals, things, places and events. As they grow,
they watch and listen to what is happening around them. And they respond – they squeal and shout, and
learn to talk; they jiggle, bounce and clap; they smile and laugh and cry. Then those around them talk back.
The exchange continues, and so as babies grow they learn more and more about their world.

Let's Go, Baby-o! is a story for parents, grandparents, teachers and childcare educators to share with babies
and little children. When you are reading the book, chant and dance the rhythms. Stop, and take time to look
out the window. Ask the question: 'What can you see in the garden?' You can also ask: 'Where is…? Can you
find…? What is…doing?' Together, follow the story of the birds as they grow up and fly away. You can also
make up your own chants and movements, and explore and name the world around you, wherever you are.

JANET MCLEAN

Let's Go, Baby-o!

Janet & Andrew McLean

ALLEN&UNWIN

Let's go, baby-o, baby-o, baby-o.
Let's go, baby-o, you and me.

To the up,
To the down,
To the turn around.

up,
down,
turn
around

Look out the window.
What can you see?

Let's go, baby-o,
you and me.
To the wibble,
To the wobble,
To the cha-cha-cha.

cha-cha-cha

Look out the window.
What can you see?

Let's go, baby-o,
you and me.
To the bounce,
To the bounce,
To the pounce-pounce-pounce.

grrr!
pounce!

Look out the window.
What can you see?

Let's go, baby-o,
you and me.
To the jump,
To the bump,
To the thump-thump-thump.

Look out the window.
What can you see?

Let's go, baby-o, you and me.
To the flip,
To the flop,
To the hop-hop-hop.

hop
hop
hop

Look out the window.
What can you see?

Let's go, baby-o,
you and me.
To the clap,
To the clap,
To the flap-flap-flap.

flap
flap flap

Look out the window.
What can you see?

Let's go, baby-o,
one more time.
To the twist,
To the twirl,
To the whirl-whirl-whirl.

twwwirl

Look out the window.
What can you see?

JANET and ANDREW MCLEAN have created a number of popular and award-winning
picture books together, including *Hector and Maggie*, *Dog Tales*, *Cat's Whiskers* and *Josh*.

Janet McLean is an early childhood educator. She has a special interest in the development of language
in young children, and would like to inspire confidence in new parents, grandparents, teachers
and childcare educators as they help children develop communication and literacy skills.

Andrew McLean is an artist and illustrator. He has taught painting, drawing and art, but is now a full-time painter
and illustrator of children's books. Many of the books illustrated by Andrew have received awards from the Children's
Book Council of Australia. *My Dog*, written by John Heffernan, won Book of the Year for Younger Readers;
You'll Wake the Baby by Catherine Jinks, and *A Year on Our Farm* by Penny Matthews, won the Book of the Year
award in the Early Childhood category. Other books illustrated by Andrew include *Reggie, Queen of the Street*
by Margaret Barbalet, *There's a Goat in my Coat* by Rosemary Milne, and *My Country* by Dorothea Mackellar.

First published in 2011

Allen & Unwin
83 Alexander Street
Crows Nest NSW 2065 Australia
Phone: (61 2) 8425 0100
Fax: (61 2) 9906 2218
Email: info@allenandunwin.com
Web: www.allenandunwin.com

A Cataloguing-in-Publication entry is available from
the National Library of Australia
www.trove.nla.gov.au

ISBN 978 174237 564 9

Cover and text design by Sandra Nobes
Set in 24 pt Bembo by Sandra Nobes
This book was printed in April 2011 at Tien Wah Press (PTE) Limited,
4 Pandan Crescent, Singapore 128475

1 3 5 7 9 10 8 6 4 2